D0597477

Mega Military Machines™

TANKS

Catherine Ellis

PowerKiDS press™

New York

Published in 2007 by The Rosen Publishing Group, Inc.
29 East 21st Street, New York, NY 10010

First Edition

Editor: Amelie von Zumbusch
Book Design: Greg Tucker

Photo Credits: Cover, p. 21 © Eugene Mogilnikov; p. 5 © Scott Nelson/Getty Images; p. 7 © Menahem Kahana/AFP/Getty Images; pp. 9, 15 © Larry W. Smith/Getty Images; p. 11 © Sgt. Paula Taylor; p. 13 © Spc. Danielle Howard; p. 17 Shutterstock.com; p. 19 © PHAN Sarah E. Ard, USN; p. 23 © Suzanne M. Day.

Library of Congress Cataloging-in-Publication Data

Ellis, Catherine.
   Tanks / Catherine Ellis. — 1st ed.
      p. cm. — (Mega military machines)
   Includes index.
   ISBN-13: 978-1-4042-3664-6 (library binding)
   ISBN-10: 1-4042-3664-3 (library binding)
   1. Tanks (Military science)—Juvenile literature. I. Title.
   UG446.5.E423 2007
   623.7'4752—dc22
                                                2006029636

Manufactured in the United States of America

Contents

People in the military drive tanks. They use tanks to fight and to move around.

Tanks have **tracks**. A tank's tracks let it be driven on or off the road.

Tanks are strong. They have **armor** on their sides to keep them safe.

Tanks have guns on them. The guns on tanks are often very big.

Soldiers ride inside of a tank. They sometimes sit so that they can look out of the top of the tank.

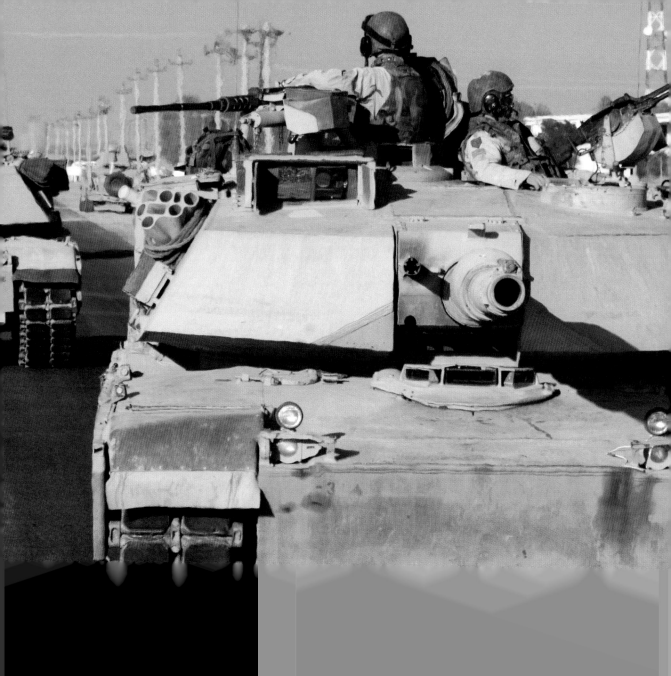

This tank is called a Bradley tank. It lets soldiers move around safely.

15

This is an M1A1 Abrams tank. The U.S. Army uses a lot of M1A1 Abrams tanks.

All tanks can be driven on land. Some tanks can go into the water, too!

Tanks come in many sizes.
This small tank can hold
three soldiers.

Tanks are often part of a **platoon**. There are three or four tanks in each platoon.

23

Words to Know

armor (AR-mer) A hard cover put over something to keep it safe.

platoon (PLUH-toon) A small military group.

soldiers (SOHL-jurz) People who are in the army.

tracks (TRAKS) The heavy bands that move a tank along.

Index

Web Sites

Due to the changing nature of Internet links, PowerKids Press has developed an online list of Web sites related to this book. This site is updated regularly. Please use this link to access the list:
www.powerkidslinks.com/mmm/tanks/

24